P9-BHR-023

HOOP DOCTOR

BY JAKE MADDOX

illustrated by Tuesday Mourning

text by Emma Carlson Berne

WITHDRAWN

STONE ARCH BOOKS
www.stonearchbooks.com

Impact Books are published by Stone Arch Books
151 Good Counsel Drive, P.O. Box 669
Mankato, Minnesota 56002
www.stonearchbooks.com

Copyright © 2010 by Stone Arch Books

All rights reserved. No part of this publication may be reproduced
in whole or in part, or stored in a retrieval system, or transmitted in any
form or by any means, electronic, mechanical, photocopying, recording,
or otherwise, without written permission of the publisher.

Library of Congress Cataloging-in-Publication Data
Maddox, Jake.
 Hoop doctor / by Jake Maddox ; text by Emma Carlson Berne ;
illustrated by Tuesday Mourning.
     p. cm. — (Impact books. A Jake Maddox sports story)
  ISBN 978-1-4342-1605-2
 [1. Basketball—Fiction.] I. Berne, Emma Carlson. II. Mourning,
Tuesday, ill. III. Title.
  PZ7.M25643Hoo 2010
  [Fic]—dc22
                              2009004079

Summary:
Kelcey wants to quit the basketball team. A mysterious person named
Dr. C is running a basketball clinic at her school. Dr. C claims to be
able to fix basketball problems, but Kelcey is sure it'll take more than a
doctor to make her love the game again.

Creative Director: Heather Kindseth
Graphic Designer: Emily Harris

Photo Credit: Shutterstock Images/ Dennis Tokarzewski, cover
(background)

Printed in the United States of America

TABLE OF CONTENTS

★ Chapter 1 ★

KELSEY'S SECRET

BEEP! As the buzzer sounded, the ball dropped through the basket for the last time. Girls jumped off the bench and poured onto the court. They were all cheering. At one end of the gym, the scoreboard read, "Tigers, 45 – Raiders, 43."

The tall girl who had made the final basket stood in the middle of the court. She smiled as the Tigers quickly surrounded her. The Raiders filed off the court.

Kelsey Peters, still panting from the game, stood by herself. She watched her teammates celebrate, her hands hanging limply at her sides. Then she turned and slowly walked toward the locker room.

"Hey, Kelsey, where are you going?" one of the girls shouted. "Your sister just won the game for us! We're going to the regional championships!"

Kelsey looked back and gave the group a little wave. Then she pushed open the door of the locker room and let it swing shut behind her.

The room was quiet. She could hardly hear the noise from the gym. Kelsey sat down on one of the benches and rested her head in her hands. She knew that her sister, Erin, would wonder where she was, but she didn't care.

Kelsey was just glad the last regular game of the season was over.

Just one more game, Kelsey told herself. *One more.* No one knew that she was going to quit basketball forever after the regional championships were over. It was her secret.

Kelsey opened her locker. *Wham!* The locker room door slammed open so hard that it banged against the wall. Kelsey started stuffing her things into her gym bag. Then a girl with dark curly hair bounded into the room.

"Hey!" Kelsey's best friend, Liz, said. "I was looking for you. Why are you in here all by yourself?"

"Oh, um, I had to go to the bathroom," Kelsey mumbled. She couldn't tell Liz her secret. Not yet.

Liz gave Kelsey a long look. Then she asked, "Wasn't Erin's shot at the end incredible? Your sister is so good, Kels. We're going to kill them at regional championships next week."

"Yeah," Kelsey said, hitching her bag over her shoulder. "It'll be great."

"Come on," Liz said. "Coach Heck is taking us all out for pizza to celebrate our win."

Kelsey hesitated. "I don't know if I really feel like it," she said.

"What?" Liz asked. "How can you not feel like pizza?"

Kelsey stared down at her shoes. Then she looked up and managed to smile at Liz, who was still staring at her. "You're right," Kelsey said. "Let's go celebrate."

✦ Chapter 2 ✦

THE NEW CENTER

The pizza restaurant was noisy and crowded. All the players gathered around a long table at the back of the room. When everyone was seated, Coach Heck stood up.

"Players!" he called. "Can I have your attention, please?"

Everyone stopped talking. The coach went on. "As you know, today was our last game of the regular season. Thanks to our center, Erin, the game was a great success."

All the girls cheered.

"We're also going to have to say goodbye to Erin after the regional championships," Coach Heck said.

"Don't leave us!" yelled Liz. She was the team's clown, always trying to get a laugh.

Coach Heck smiled. "She'll be graduating and heading off to high school," he said. Everyone groaned.

Kelsey watched her tall sister, seated at the head of the table, smiling modestly. Erin had been the star player on the Tigers for the last three seasons. She was famous for her speed and jumps.

Liz leaned over. "I can't even imagine the Tigers without Erin," she whispered to Kelsey. "What are we going to do without her?"

Coach Heck was still talking. "Luckily, we have someone else on the team who can continue Erin's legacy. Someone who shows the same commitment and dedication to her team."

All the girls glanced around the table and whispered to each other.

Kelsey and Liz looked at one another. "Who's he talking about?" Liz whispered. Kelsey shrugged her shoulders. She had no idea.

"Kelsey Peters! Please stand up!" Coach Heck declared.

What? Kelsey thought. *Not me! Anyone but me!*

She looked around the table. Everyone was smiling and clapping. Slowly, she got to her feet. Erin gave her a big grin.

"Kelsey, starting next season, we're moving you from guard to center, just like your sister. We're glad you're here to take her place," said the coach.

All the Tigers cheered. Liz put her fingers in her mouth and whistled. Erin stood up and came around the table.

"You've got to carry on the Peters legacy, sis," Erin said, hugging her sister.

Kelsey stood completely still. Her heart felt like it had fallen right out of her chest and into her shoes. To her horror, she felt tears starting in her eyes.

She broke out of her sister's grasp and ran to the restroom. Behind her, she could hear the clapping stop.

★ Chapter 3 ★

BASKETBALL WIZARD

Kelsey leaned against one of the sinks in the empty restroom. She watched in the mirror as a few tears rolled down her cheeks. She could hear Liz and Erin talking just outside the door.

Why can't they just leave me alone? she thought.

"What's up with her?" Erin asked.

"I'm not sure, but I think I should go in by myself," Liz said.

Erin was quiet for a second. "Okay, if you think so," she said finally. "Just come get me if she needs me."

"Okay," Liz said. Then she pushed the door open. "Kels, what's the matter?" she asked. "Why are you crying?"

Kelsey stared down at the sink. She'd never told anyone her secret before. But now she felt like she was going to burst if she didn't say something. She looked at her friend and took a deep breath.

"Liz, I have something to tell you," Kelsey said.

"What?" Liz asked. She put her arm around Kelsey's shoulders. "What's wrong?"

"I . . . I don't want to be center next season. Actually, I don't want to play basketball ever again," Kelsey said.

She looked down at her feet. She couldn't stand to see Liz staring at her.

"Why, Kels? Is it Coach Heck?" Liz asked.

"No, Coach Heck is fine," Kelsey said. "I guess I'm just sort of sick of it."

Liz was quiet for a minute. "Wow," she finally said. "I'm confused. I mean, you're really good. Why don't you like playing basketball anymore?"

Kelsey sighed. "I'm not sure I ever liked it. It just always seemed like something I was expected to do," she explained.

"You mean, because your sister always played?" Liz asked.

"Yeah," Kelsey said. "So everyone, including Coach Heck and my parents, just expected that I would play too."

"But you're an awesome player," Liz said.

Kelsey slid down the wall until she was sitting on the floor. She looped her arms around her knees and laid her head on them. "Thanks," she said. "But you have to believe me, Liz, whenever I'm playing, it doesn't feel like fun. It just feels like some kind of chore I have to do."

Liz sat down on the floor next to her friend. "I think you should tell Coach Heck you don't want to play next season," she said. "He's already talking about how we might make it to the championship again with you as the new center."

"No!" Kelsey yelled, sitting up straight. "I can't tell him. I can't disappoint everyone like that. They all think I love basketball as much as Erin does."

Both girls were quiet for a minute, thinking. Then Liz held up her finger. "Hey!" she said. "I just thought of something to help you."

"A permanent vacation in Jamaica?" Kelsey asked gloomily.

"No, look," Liz said. She fished a wadded piece of paper out of her pocket. "Coach Heck handed these out right after the game, when you were in the locker room." She handed the paper to Kelsey.

Dr. C, Basketball Wizard! proclaimed huge letters at the top of the flyer. *Cures for all your basketball woes! Dribbling, passing, shooting, speed, agility, and jumping. Let Dr. C diagnose you, treat you, and cure you!*

Clinic: 9-12, Saturday, June 1, Longbranch Middle School Gymnasium.

Dr. C
Basketball Wizard!

Cures for all your
basketball woes!
Dribbling, passing,
shooting, speed,
agility, and
jumping.
Let Dr. C
diagnose you,
treat you, and
cure you!

Clinic: 9-12, Saturday,
June 1, Longbranch
Middle School Gymnasium.

"It's at our school!" Liz said. "On Saturday."

Kelsey stared at the paper for a minute and then shoved it back to Liz. "This guy isn't going to help me," she said. "This is just a basketball clinic. We have them all the time, remember? These coaches just come in and help you work on your free throw, or whatever."

"I know, but this Dr. C seems different. He's an expert on basketball problems," Liz said, pointing to the flyer. "You need some help, Kels. Maybe this guy can cure you." She reached over and stuffed the paper into Kelsey's pocket. "You should go."

Kelsey heaved herself up from the floor and pulled Liz up too. "Thanks," Kelsey said. "But I think the only thing that can help me is quitting basketball forever."

Chapter 4

AN EXTRA PRACTICE

All week, whenever Kelsey thought about the upcoming championship game on Monday, she felt like she was going to throw up. Even seeing a game on television sent her stomach churning.

When Coach Heck called an extra practice on Friday afternoon, Kelsey felt like hiding under her bed. Instead, she got out her basketball shoes and forced herself to head for the gym.

Erin was already there, and so was the rest of the team. Coach Heck set everyone up to practice passing. As Kelsey passed the ball to her partner over and over, she kept telling herself, *Just one more game, just one more game.*

"All right, players, let's get ready for a scrimmage," Coach Heck called out. "We need to be in top form for Monday."

Erin raised her hand. "Coach, do you mind if I sit this one out?" she asked. "My knee is bothering me a little. It'll probably feel better if I rest it." The coach nodded, and Erin trotted over to the bleachers.

During the scrimmage, Kelsey tried to concentrate on passing and dribbling. But all she could think about was finishing practice so she could get out of there, off the court and away from the gym.

She passed and blocked like a robot, barely listening to Coach Heck's shouted instructions. But then, near the end of the scrimmage, someone passed her the ball, and it thumped into her hands with a solid *thwack*!

For a minute, everything around her disappeared. All Kelsey saw was the basket, open in front of her.

Without thinking, she dribbled the ball up the court, fast. The basket was open. She jumped high and shot. The ball slammed through the net.

The players around her cheered as Kelsey's sneakers landed back onto the court. Coach Heck was clapping from the sidelines. "Nice work, Erin!" he yelled. "Sorry, I meant Kelsey!"

No one else seemed to notice Coach's slip-up, not even Erin. But Kelsey felt a weight thump down on her stomach.

Bam. Just like that, the good feelings from making the basket were gone.

✦ Chapter 5 ✦

LESS BASKETBALL

After the practice, Coach Heck called everyone into a huddle. The girls crowded around him, panting and tired. He flipped to a new page on his clipboard.

"All right, Tigers," he said. "I need to know who's coming to the special Dr. C clinic on Saturday. This is going to be a once-in-a-lifetime chance to work with this world-famous coach, so I'd encourage you all to show up."

He raised his pen over his clipboard. "So, who's in?" he asked.

Hands shot up, and the coach started scribbling names down. Kelsey kept her arms at her sides.

Coach Heck looked up. "Who else? Kelsey?" he asked.

"Um, I have a dentist appointment," Kelsey mumbled. She felt Liz elbow her in the ribs.

"Oh, Kelsey," Liz said loudly. "I just remembered. Your mom wanted me to tell you that your dentist broke both his arms, so your appointment is canceled!"

Kelsey glared at her friend who gave her an innocent smile. Coach Heck looked confused. "Okay, so Kelsey's in, is that right?" he asked.

"That's right!" Liz said. Kelsey kicked her friend's ankle.

"Great!" the coach said, scribbling on his clipboard. "That's it. Get a good night's sleep, girls, and we'll see you all tomorrow."

The team scattered to the locker room, but Kelsey pulled Liz to a quiet spot under the bleachers. "Why did you do that?" she asked angrily.

Liz widened her eyes. "What are you talking about? You mean your dentist didn't break both arms?" she asked.

Kelsey gritted her teeth. "Drop it, Liz," she said. "You know I don't want to go to the clinic. I need less basketball in my life, not more."

"I'm sorry," Liz said. "I just think that this guy could help you."

"Well, he can't!" Kelsey snapped. A hot wave of anger rushed over her. "I told you, I don't want to play anymore. Not tomorrow, not next season. Maybe not ever!" She picked up her bag and stormed away, ignoring the hurt look on Liz's face.

✦ Chapter 6 ✦

MEETING MARIAN

Kelsey pushed through the heavy double doors of the gym and rushed into the bright, blinding sunlight. Her chest felt tight, and her head was pounding.

She wove her way through the cars in the school parking lot, fighting to keep the tears from rolling down her face. She was trying so hard not to cry that she ran right into the tall woman getting out of a car in front of her.

"Ooof!" Kelsey said, stumbling. She dropped her stack of books and her gym bag flew off her shoulder. It hit the ground, and the zipper split, spilling her uniform, socks, and basketball shoes all over the ground. The tall woman caught her by the shoulders before she fell.

"Sorry about that!" the woman said. "Are you okay?"

Kelsey looked up — way up. The woman towered over her. She was smiling down at Kelsey through round glasses. "I was looking at my directions instead of watching where I was going," the woman said. She was holding a piece of paper in her hand.

"Oh. It's okay," Kelsey told her. She crouched down and started collecting her books.

"Your stuff went everywhere!" the woman said, kneeling and gathering up Kelsey's gym socks. "Here you go. I'm Marian, by the way."

"I'm Kelsey," Kelsey mumbled without looking up. She concentrated on collecting papers from her math binder, but she could feel Marian looking at her.

"If you don't mind my saying so, you seemed pretty upset a moment ago," Marian said.

Kelsey looked up, startled. She was surprised that an adult had noticed how she was feeling. She hesitated a moment and then shrugged. "I'm okay," she said.

Marian picked up the last few scattered papers. She turned one over and studied it for a minute before handing it to Kelsey.

It was the clinic flyer. "Basketball clinic tomorrow, huh?" Marian asked. "Who's Dr. C?"

"I don't know," Kelsey said. "Some kind of basketball doctor. He says he can cure all your problems. But I'm not going." She stuffed the paper into her backpack. "He can't cure the kind of problems I have."

Marian paused for a moment and then nodded. "Yeah," she said. "It probably wouldn't be worth the time. Hey, I have an appointment here at the gym, and I'm a few minutes early. Would you mind showing me the way?"

"Sure," Kelsey said, rising to her feet. She didn't really feel like going back into the school, but she knew the other Tigers would already be gone. She'd show Marian where the gym was and then go home.

"It's through those doors and down the hall," Kelsey said.

Kelsey led Marian into the building. The big, echoing gym was deserted. But the lights were still on, so Kelsey knew Coach Heck was around somewhere. He always turned the lights off as he was leaving.

"Here you are," Kelsey said.

"Thanks, Kelsey," Marian replied. "I appreciate it."

Kelsey turned to go. She stopped when she heard the squeak of shoes on the court behind her. She turned around.

Marian had picked up a basketball and was dribbling up and down the court. Kelsey caught her breath. She'd never seen anyone run like that before. It was like she was flying above the floor.

As Kelsey watched, Marian jumped into the air and flew toward the basket. She dropped the ball through the net as if the basket were only three feet off the ground.

Kelsey couldn't believe what she was seeing. She stood rooted to the ground as Marian dribbled down to the other end of the court. This time, she leaped toward the net and dunked the ball from under and around the basket.

"Wow!" Kelsey blurted out. Marian stopped and turned toward her. She looked surprised to see Kelsey still standing there.

"Like that move?" Marian asked, smiling a little. "I worked on that one for about two years."

"It was awesome!" Kelsey said, throwing down her backpack. "How did you do it?"

"Ah, that's a signature move," Marian said, winking. "I never reveal my secrets."

"You've got to tell me!" Kelsey insisted.

Marian studied her for a moment. "Go change into your practice clothes. I'll have to see you play first," she said. "I don't reveal my secrets to just anyone."

✦ Chapter 7 ✦

BASKETBALL PROBLEMS

"I'm ready," Kelsey said, opening her hands for the ball. Marian passed it to her, and she caught it solidly against her chest.

"All right, let's see you dribble," Marian said. "I'm going to guard you."

Kelsey started dribbling up the court.

"So," Marian said, easily running in front of her, "what's with these basketball problems of yours? I have to say, you look pretty comfortable on the court."

Kelsey shrugged and did a lay-up. "It's nothing," she said. "I'm just sick of playing."

"Why don't you quit?" Marian asked. She stole the ball and ran up the court to the other basket. Kelsey ran after her. She waved her arms, trying to block Marian's shot.

"I don't know," Kelsey said. "I think maybe I'm going to. But . . ."

She paused, watching Marian shoot. When she took a shot, the ball seemed to float through the basket.

"It's just that everyone's going to be so mad," Kelsey said. "My parents, Coach Heck, Erin . . ."

"Who's Erin?" Marian asked. She handed Kelsey the ball. "Try some spins while you dribble."

Kelsey tried an awkward spin and missed the ball. It bounced away down the court.

"Erin's my sister," she said after she retrieved the ball. "She's been the center on the team for years."

"So why does she care if you play basketball?" Marian asked. She took the ball from Kelsey and did three spins while dribbling.

"Keep your eyes in one spot while you spin," Marian said, handing the ball back. "That's the key."

Kelsey spun again. This time, she managed to keep the ball under control.

"It's just that everyone wants me to be exactly like her," Kelsey explained. "They even call me Erin sometimes. They think we're the same person, but we're not!"

Her voice rose, and she did another spin. This time, she kept the ball in play perfectly.

"You've got it!" Marian said. "That was it, the way you just did it."

Kelsey stopped. "Wow, I did it!" she said.

Marian grinned. "All right, let's see you shoot," she said.

Kelsey dribbled the ball down the court and tossed the ball toward the basket.

"Hmm," Marian said. "If you shoot like that all the time, you won't have to worry about people caring if you quit. That was awful. Your sister must shoot better than that."

Kelsey felt a bubble of anger rise in her chest. Another person was comparing her to Erin. And Marian didn't even know her!

Marian came close and stared right into Kelsey's face. "What are you playing for, Kelsey?" she asked in a low voice. "If you don't want to play basketball, then don't. But if you're on this court, then respect the game."

"I want to play!" Kelsey almost shouted. "You don't even know me, so don't pretend like you know about my problems!"

Marian shoved the ball at her. "Then play!" she said. She turned her back and walked to the edge of the court.

★ Chapter 8 ★

PLAYING WITH FIRE

Kelsey was so mad, the whole world looked blurry. Who did Marian think she was, telling her she didn't respect the game?

She wanted to throw the ball right at the back of Marian's head. Instead, she turned and dribbled up the court.

I'll show her, Kelsey thought. *I'll show her she doesn't know anything about me.*

Kelsey reached the end of the court. Her steps were in perfect rhythm with the ball.

Without thinking, she spun, jumped, and shot the ball. She caught it on the rebound, and dribbled back down to the other end of the court fast.

Suddenly, she heard Marian from the sidelines. "Respect the game!" she shouted. "Respect the game!"

I do! Kelsey thought furiously. She leaped through the air and slammed the ball toward the basket. Then her sneakers hit the court floor again.

Kelsey let the ball roll into a corner of the gym. Then she turned to the sidelines, panting.

To her surprise, a huge grin was plastered across Marian's face. Slowly and loudly clapping her hands, she walked toward Kelsey.

"Well, that was very nice," Marian said, still grinning. "That was quite a shot at the end. In a few years, you could probably learn to dunk."

"Wow," Kelsey said. "Really?" She knew that being able to dunk was rare in women's basketball.

"I can see something special in you, Kelsey," Marian added. "You just haven't been playing with any fire in your belly. You've been getting out there on that court and thinking, *I hate this game, I'll never be as good as my sister.* You weren't remembering the best part of basketball. The best part is playing with a little feeling and having fun."

"But I don't even like basketball," Kelsey argued.

Marian waved her hand. "Yeah, you do," she said. "You just don't like following your sister's shadow around. So use those feelings. Take whatever you're feeling and play your game with it. Whatever it takes just to get out there on the court and get that ball in the basket."

Just then, Coach Heck walked into the gym from his office. "I thought I heard voices out here," he said, coming toward them and smiling. "Dr. C! It's so great to see you again!" He shook Marian's hand. "Kelsey, I see you've met Dr. Marian Clark."

Kelsey gasped. "You're Dr. C?" she asked. "But I thought Dr. C was a man!"

Marian smiled. "Guess again," she said. "Not all great basketball players are men, you know."

"Oh, yeah, right," Kelsey replied slowly. "Um, well, thanks for the lesson, Dr. C."

Marian smiled. "Anytime," she said. "Good luck in the championship game on Monday."

Kelsey left. She slowly walked home, thinking about everything that had happened on the court.

It had been the first time she'd played without thinking about how much she didn't want to be there. And the feeling of flying toward the basket . . . that had been pretty incredible.

Kelsey started walking up the sidewalk to her house. The front door was partly open, which was odd. Mom was strict about keeping it closed. Then she noticed something blue lying on the lawn.

As Kelsey got nearer, she could see that it was Erin's backpack. Kelsey frowned. Why had her sister just left her bag in the middle of the grass like that?

Kelsey ran up the front steps and opened the screen door. "Mom?" she called as she put her things down in the front hall.

Her mother's voice came from the living room. "In here, Kelsey," she said.

Kelsey walked around the corner and stopped. Erin was sitting in the recliner, crying, and their mother was kneeling on the floor in front of her.

"Bad news, sweetie," Mom said. "Erin sprained her wrist. She tripped coming up the steps outside."

Kelsey's mouth fell open. "But the big game is on Monday!" she exclaimed.

Even though she hated to admit it, she was worried about the team. She didn't want everyone to be disappointed. And she felt terrible for her sister. The championship game was the biggest one of the year.

Erin forced a smile even though she was in pain. "Mom," she said. "Say hello to the Tigers' new center: Kelsey Peters."

✦ Chapter 9 ✦

USE IT!

Kelsey laced up her basketball shoes. Then she rested her arms on her knees for a moment, letting her head dangle.

Her heart was pounding so hard, she thought it might burst out of her chest and fly across the room. She tried to take deep breaths, but she couldn't calm down.

All around her, the Tigers were pulling on their uniforms. The girls were shouting to each other and laughing.

The regional championship game against the Rams was supposed to start in five minutes. Everyone was excited.

Next to Kelsey, Liz was struggling with a knot in her shoelace. "Stupid lace!" she muttered, her hair falling over her eyes. She looked up. "You're so quiet, Kels!" she told her friend. "Are you sad this is our last game of the year?"

Kelsey shook her head. "I don't know what I am. I'm scared, I guess. I've never started at center before."

Liz nodded. "I know. You're like the star of the game, and it hasn't even started yet!" she said, smiling.

"Thanks a lot," Kelsey said. "Now I'm even more nervous!"

* * *

Kelsey could hear the noise of the crowd even before she stepped onto the court. The stands were packed, but all the faces looked like one big blur.

She heard Erin's voice from the stands. "Go, Tigers!" Erin yelled.

Kelsey looked up into the bleachers. Her sister was sitting with their mom.

Erin's hand was wrapped in bandages, but she was smiling happily and waving at Kelsey and their other teammates. Kelsey realized that this was the first game she'd ever played without Erin.

On my own, she thought. *I'm on my own for the first time.*

A feeling of lightness flooded her, and she suddenly heard Dr. C's voice in her head.

"Take whatever you're feeling and play your game with it," Dr. C had said. "Whatever it takes just to get out there on the court and get that ball in the basket."

When she'd played with Dr. C., Kelsey had felt mad. But now she didn't feel angry. She felt excited. Happy, almost. *Then use it!* Dr. C insisted from inside Kelsey's head.

All right, Kelsey thought. *I will.*

She reached up, tightened her ponytail, and jogged onto the court to join the huddle. "Go, Tigers!" she yelled as she came up to the other girls.

Coach Heck gave everyone a few last instructions, and before Kelsey could think, the buzzer sounded. The championship game had begun.

✦ Chapter 10 ✦

THE PETERS LEGACY

Kelsey dribbled the ball up the court, then shot it fast to Liz, who was open. Liz took it up to the basket, but the guard was on her by then.

"Here, Liz!" Kelsey shouted. The ball thumped into her hands. She leaped for the basket, just managing to tip it in.

"Nice, Kelsey!" Coach Heck shouted. A couple of Tigers applauded as everyone ran down the court.

Lightness, Kelsey thought. *Use it!* And as someone passed her the ball again, she felt the lightness flood her body.

The opposing guard was blocking her, but she spun, still dribbling the ball. She easily darted past the guard.

Lightness! she thought again.

As Kelsey lunged at the basket, her feet felt like they'd grown wings. She eyed the basket and leaped. The ball slammed through the net.

The Tigers erupted in screams as Kelsey's feet hit the court. Kelsey caught a glimpse of Coach Heck standing perfectly still on the sidelines, his mouth hanging open.

The rest of the game was a blur of squeaking sneakers, breathless shouts, sweat, and the thump of the ball.

Again and again, Kelsey put the ball through the net. Her mind was empty of any thoughts except the feel of the ball in her hands and the pounding of her feet on the court. When the final buzzer sounded, the score was 35–20, Tigers.

Coach Heck ran out onto the floor and was immediately swarmed by his shouting players. Everyone was talking at once and high-fiving each other.

Then the coach held up his hand. "Girls! What a game!" said Coach Heck. "I think we need a special round of applause for the top player of the game, our new center, Kelsey Peters! How did you do it, Kelsey?"

Kelsey smiled. "I just played with whatever I had in me," she said.

* * *

Later, Liz and Kelsey walked home together.

"I thought you didn't like basketball," Liz said. "What happened?"

"I didn't think I did," Kelsey said. She stopped walking and looked down. "But now I think what I really didn't like was playing in my sister's shadow. Now that she's gone, I feel like I can, I don't know, be myself on the court. Instead of being a little Erin, I can just play however I feel like playing that day."

"So, you're not quitting?" Liz asked. She looked confused.

Kelsey grinned and draped an arm around her friend's shoulder as they started walking again. "Nope. Looks like the Peters legacy is going to live on."

★ ABOUT THE AUTHOR ★

Emma Carlson Berne has written more than a dozen books for children and young adults, including teen romance novels, biographies, and history books. She lives in Cincinnati, Ohio with her husband, Aaron, her son, Henry, and her dog, Holly.

★ ABOUT THE ILLUSTRATOR ★

When Tuesday Mourning was a little girl, she knew she wanted to be an artist when she grew up. Now, she is an illustrator who lives in South Pasadena, CA. She especially loves illustrating books for kids and teenagers. When she isn't illustrating, Tuesday loves spending time with her husband, who is an actor, and their two sons.

★ GLOSSARY ★

championship (CHAM-pee-uhn-ship)—a contest determining which team will be the final winner

commitment (kuh-MIT-muhnt)—a promise to do something

cure (KYUR)—to fix something

dedication (ded-uh-KAY-shun)—devotion or concentration of effort

diagnose (dye-uhg-NOHSS)—determine what the cause of a problem is

legacy (LEG-uh-see)—what someone is known for

modestly (MOD-ist-lee)—without bragging

regional (REE-juhn-uhl)—of one area

regular (REG-yuh-lur)—usual or normal

scrimmage (SKRIM-ij)—a game played for practice

woes (WOHZ)—troubles or problems

FUN BASKETBALL GAMES YOU CAN PLAY

Basketball is fun, but what do you do when you don't have enough players or time to play a full game? Don't give up — there are lots of ways to play even when you don't have two full teams. Here are just a few ideas.

HORSE can be played with two or more players. To play, one player shoots from anywhere on the court. If that player makes the shot, the other players must also shoot from the same spot. Any player who doesn't make the shot gets a letter from the word **HORSE**. Once a player has all of the letters, he or she is out of the game. The winner is the person left when everyone else is out.

PIG is a shorter variation of **HORSE**. Play it when you don't have enough time to play a full game of **HORSE**.

AROUND THE WORLD can be played with two or more players. To play, each player makes a shot from set points around the key on the court. The first person to make it "around the world" wins. For another variation of this game, start right in front of the hoop, and then step backward after each shot is made. The first player to make it to half-court wins.

TWENTY-ONE requires at least two players, but is more fun with three or more. In this game, each player is on his or her own team and keeps his or her own score. No player ever has a teammate, but everyone must work together to keep each player from scoring. The first player to 21 is the winner.

★ DISCUSSION QUESTIONS ★

1. Many people try to support and help Kelsey in this book. Who are they? What do they do? What are some other things a friend could do to help Kelsey?

2. Why does Kelsey want to stop playing basketball?

3. What do you think would have happened if Kelsey hadn't met Marian? Talk about different things that could have happened.

★ WRITING PROMPTS ★

1. Kelsey is tired of being compared to her sister. Write about your sibling. What is he or she like? In what ways are you alike? If you don't have a sibling, write about a cousin, friend, or neighbor.

2. Dr. C helps Kelsey. Write about an adult who has helped you. What did he or she do to help?

3. What do you think happens after this book ends? Write another chapter that picks up where this book leaves off.

SPORTS STORIES
FOR EVERY ATHLETE

BY JAKE MADDOX

READ THEM ALL!

WAIT!

DON'T close the book!
There's MORE!

FIND MORE:
Games
Puzzles
Heroes
Villains
Authors
Illustrators at...

www.**capstonekids**.com

Still want MORE?
Find cool websites and more books like this
one at www.Facthound.com.

Just type in the Book ID: 9781434216052
and you're ready to go!

3 1901 04901 5110